8TH GRADE SEX ED QUESTIONS

CINDY TOMLINSON

INTRODUCTION

"How does the peanut get into the vagina?"

This is the question that led me to two realizations. One, that I needed to work on my enunciation, since my students believed me to be saying "peanut" every time I said "penis"! And two, that I should begin saving the students' questions for a future comical book.

Fast-forward thirty years, and voila! The following pages are a compilation of my 8th graders' sex ed questions that I have reconstructed for this publication.

I started teaching Sex Education in the mid-1980s. It didn't take me long to realize that the students were embarrassed to ask questions aloud. I brought in a shoe box and labeled it "The Question Box." Students would take the last three or four minutes of class to write down their anonymous question and drop it in the shoe box upon exiting class. The following day I would answer their questions. (The best I could, considering what I was being asked, ha ha ha.)

As I collected more and more questions, I would occasionally take them out to share with friends and family. No matter how many times I took the questions out, they never failed to have us doubled over and rolling on the floor with uncontrollable laughter.

It's the perfect book to bring along on vacation, take out at a bachelorette party, or have available on a camping or road trip.

Here are a few ways you can enjoy the book:

1. Just pick up the book anytime you're in need of a good chuckle.
2. Pass it around the room at a party or gathering. When the book lands in your hands, it's your turn to read aloud the questions on that page.
3. Put friends on the spot by asking *them* to answer the question! How this works: the person with the book in hand calls out someone's name in the group. Then the person with the book proceeds to read a question and the person they named must answer it!
4. Make up your own game with your own set of rules!

You can pull this book out again and again and find new things to giggle about each time. Believe it or not, you might even learn something.

Enjoy!

Cindy

Why do girls wipe front to back instead of back to front

What is the average size penis?

can your pubic
hairs be different
colors

Can I have AIDS
right now? Maybe I
don't know.
Maybe my mom had it?

what is oral sex?

do you think people
"those people" had SEX
with monkeys

can you get
AIV from period
blood

Why can't gays
marry?

can u get aids
by getting a
tattoo.

the manipulation for stimulation to cause fertilization is masturbation unless there's ejaculation to cause ovulation which forms our nation

DUH!

By: Sara and her table :)

why do men get "boners" when they look at hot chicks?

My penis has been the same size all my life.

Statement

What is teabag

what would you
say if someone in
here had a discharge
does the "frothy"
discharge seep out

how does a girl
put on a condom

how many sexual positions
are there, which one feels
better, and which one is
your favorite?

If guys have an orgasm to release
sperm to pregnate a woman, then why
do women have orgasms?
— Confused
Guy

what is an orgasm? In
detail

What do you mean I
Donned a girl?

Is it Normal to wake up
with a TP
~~~~~~~
~~~~~~~

Why don't they make condoms thicker so that they don't brake?

What would Bigfoots penis be like?

mrs Tomlinson-have
you ever gotten
any of these
diseases?

How does the sperm come out
the foreskin?

why is my
DICK SO BIG.!

what's morningwood?

what happens if your pants
accidentally fall of when
your with a boy?

Can A boys peanut break
A girls virginia?

IS "slong"
slang for a
short
penis

Is it true if you have a huge
Penis you will produce more sperm?

Can a girl
get preganet
by masterbatieng?

is it bad if you have
a mole on your pinus

why Ar girls near bras

How do you tell when
~~you~~ a guy and a girl are
fired while sexual intercourse

Can the nuts be on top
of the penises

why do guys get Boners?

Can girls have wet Dreams too?

How do blood vessels get soo hard?

Is it possible to have
two penises

Do girls go into
heat like dogs?

why are guys ~~so~~ so attracted to BOOBS

do guys have anything like a period?

How fast does semen come out of the Penis in Miles per hour? ⟹ → 200M

Do girls fart out of the Vagina? for real?

Can you have sex without ~~beaing~~ an erection?

Once a guy gets older, does there penis shrink or it stays the same?

what if Some Sort of Small animal were To Make the vagina their home?

when you pull out where
is the best place to ejaculate

What is
camel toe

If you have sex through
the bottle and the girl
takes 9 farts do your testicles
blow up.

what happens if a girl swallows the sperm while giving a B.J. what would happen? (blow job)

HAVE YOU EVER SEEN ANYONE WITH A CONEHEAD?

Does the size of your feet help the size of a males penis?

whats a difference from
a tampon and a pad?
and I'm REALLY Hungry
I want KFC please...!!!

is it Possible to stick your
Hole arm uP the viginia?
For real

If guys get erections, ~~how~~ what
do girls do when they get
spning?

why do girls scream
when they have sex?

Is it true that
a males pnis
is as big as
their hands?.

Do you grow
hair in the
palm of your
hand if
you master-
bate too
much?

Does seamen shoot out of the penis
during an ejaculation or does it trickle?

why would someone want
to leave the foreskin on?

Does it feel "GOOD" when the penis
enters the vagina? Does it hurt?

Is it true that if you remove the
foreskin the penis gets bigger?

Is it a sign that you have crabs if your armpits & humhum ich?

Why does it hurt when you get soap in your penis

can the foreskin on the penis grow back after the circumcision?

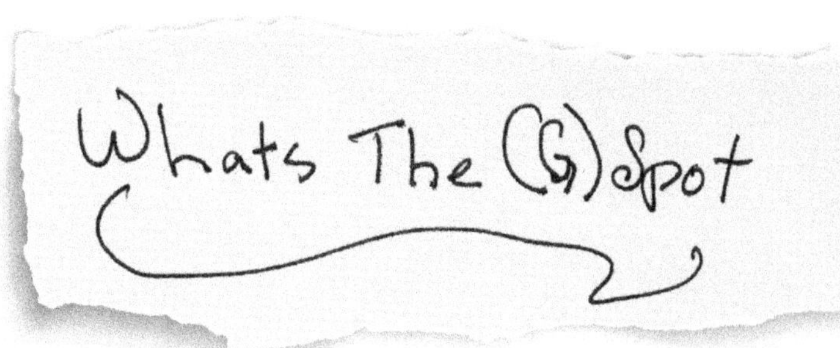

Can you still have sexual intercourse with foreskin?

Why do they make
different flavored
condoms?

Yum
trojan
lollipop

Question

* When a boy has a wet
dream do they notice?

How can Homosexurals have sexual intercourse if say they were girls. There is nothing to go into anything?

If you shave your pubic hair can you still get crabs? Can you break your cervex w/a vibrator?

if you have oral sex,
does that mean you
are not a virgin?

Why do guys scratch
the wanker?

Have you ever farted and
something comes out?

When a girl gets pregnant,
does she have to get pregnant
through the vagina or the butt?

What is the healthy amount
of times a guy should jack-off?
Love,
Mark

Why do Homosexual people
follow Me

Do you go blind if
you Masturbate?

are 3somes safe?

Does the sea section hurt more?

If you have a boner
and you are standing
behind your bedroom
door and your mom
walks in, and the
door hits your penis
will it break?

What is chaffing

Are
Donkey Punches legal
in California?

can you get pregnant
if you get sexualy active
for only like 2 seconds?
or 2 minutes

when the penis enters the
vagina, to inject the sperm
does that mean the guy
has to pee in the vagina?

Can you have sex with
a girl in &her bladder.?

If you ejackulate in a
girl can you get it
out Somehow

Can a penis crack.?
Some guys say it can
+ some say it cant

Can you brake
your vagina? It's
a serious question.

Why DO SOME people NEED
A CIGARETTE AFTER SEX?

Why is the penis hard
during an erection?

can a boy move his
penis when he wants to,
or does it just happen?
does it go up like a
slinky or slowly or fast?

What if the penis can't
fit into the vagina?

Can you urinate in an anus during anal sex?

HOW long is the normal time for inter-course?

Do U perfer big or small peniss

① Why do guys have boners every 90 min.

② Do girls get plessure while having sex.

WHY IS IT ALWAYS WARM IN GUY'S PANTS?

What ~~Deseses~~ Std's can you get From a donkey?

What does the expression
"cut the rug" with someone mean?
(something like "cut")

At what age does the
penis stop growing?

whats
a milk
shower?

Is it possible for a human to
have sex with a animal and
get it pregnant

Can your pubic hairs
be different colors?

Why do people moan when
they have sex

Is the "first time" scary?

HOW WOULD THE SPERM COMEOUT OF
THE FORESKIN

How big are Go-Nads

Why do you need wisdom
teeth to ejaculate.

Why do they call
masrurbaria Jacking-off

What is the average
size penis.

1. Can a girl get
   pregnate if you
   do her in the buthole.

Can u hide things
in your penis if
your not
     curcumzized

why do dogs "have intercourse"
with your leg?!!

Does the baby poop
or pee in the
uterus or whatever
it is in?

CAN YOU GET A CHICK
PREGNANT IF YOU BLOW
YOUR LOAD IN HER
MOUTH AND SHE SWALLOWS IT?

can you really
pop a girls
    cherry?

How come it hurts
when the penut gets
in the vigina.

51

Why am I so horny ALL
the time? I just WANt
to HAve Sex. Im a
Sexual beast.
SEX

Do girls have three
holes in ... um ...
down below her
belly button?

Can you have
too much
Masterbation?

why do I crave older women
and only older women, younger
chicks dont even make me happy

Does it hurt
from behind?

why does the vagina
get wet during sex?

If a girl goes to
the bathroom and
a guy left sperm
on the toilet and
the girl didnt
notice and sit on
the pile of sperm
is it possible to get
pregnant right there
and Also— what
is a pearl Necklace

why do girls prefer
shaving their vagina?

could you call a
"wet dream" a
"damp nightmare"?

How big is the biggest
penis on record

What would happen if a girl forgot to take off her underpants when she was having her baby

what if a guy ejaculates while at a public place, will it be noticible?

Do tampons feel weird, good, pleasurable, um?

when your pushing so hard
when you R giving a ~~baby~~,
do you have to crap ?

Could you still get
Pregnet if the guy
gets <u>nudered</u> !

What is a gang bang?
What is a tea bag?

Do frogs have sexual
intercoarse?

If a boy or a girl
gose bald will there
pubbs fall off.

why do I like
girls, guys and
animals?

Can u get pregnant
DOING IT DOGGY
STYLE? I'M NOT
trying to be funny

why do young boys
like breast so much?

Why do
Men
Jack off!?

why would someone
masterbate? I dont
understand what it is
I guess?

If a condom gets stuck
in a vagina how will
it come out

Nunchuck skills, computer
hacking skills!
Did you always feel comfortable
discussing these things?

How bout them Padres?

What is a pinocha

can you get S.T.D.
from penis sucking?

What age can we buy
a condom?

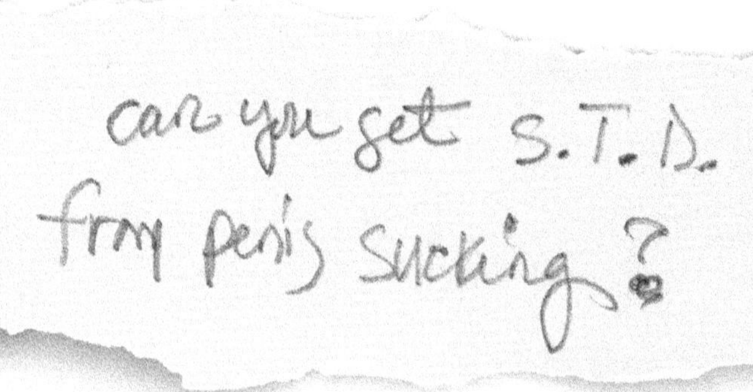

DO women use tampons
to masterbate, hmmm.

During a sexual
intercourse what
trigers your pennis
to spem?

what happens if you have
intercorse with 2
different people

can you get a disease
from Masturbation. I sure
hope not !!

I read that a
woman got pg
by her dog- so can
it be abnormal

mrs, Tomlinson - whats the biggest
penis youve ever seen?
Did you touch it

can you remove a penus
from a guy and sew it on
to a vagina then have sex
with yourself? yippie

What duse female
masterbateting fell like?
and what's a punoch

How far in does a vagina go?
In inches?
From Josh

What is the average circumference of a testicle?

Is there such a thing as a tripod (3 testes) ??

Name
different
ways to
masterbate
PLEASE

if flexible
enough, can a
man give himself
oral sex?

Why do boys get
random boners?

why do girls ~~suc~~ suck on
the penis

do geres have sperm
thet squirts out like guys?

How does a big
baby fit thru
the vagina?

can you get an
orgasm in your
breast?

How deep is
a vagina

can a man
have 3 testicles)

Is sperm bad for
you if you swallow it?

can u get pg from
butt sex.

why do people
Jack off — does
everyone do it or no?
I do :)

Is penis length determined
by height, teeth, etc.?

explain the
testicular dropping
process
(the balls dropping)

Can the penis brake?

If you ejaculate onto
a girls tummy can the
sperm swim down into
her vagina?

Are we going to watch
a video or see
~~colors~~ color pictures

what is '69'?

How do boys get
Semen places?

Can your vagina
get rusty?

How long does it take
for the vagina to go
back in regular size

Are black peoples
semen black?
or white?

why do crazy people
eat their afterbirth?

what happens when
girls get horny?

why do boys like
having sex

How do horses have sex?

I heard that if your pp is bent - don't you have a virus? 👀

What IS spooning?

Can you get sexual
diseis by Mastubation

can girls have Sex after an
orgasm? and what happens
is a male urinates in the
vagina of a succulent woman?

how come boys usually get
erections when they see
something " ~~that~~ pleasing "

Does IT hurt
the 1st time?
(It = having sex)

If you had an
erection while being
circumcised would you
bleed to death?

how far does the penis
go into the vagina
is until the penis
hits the "g-spot"?

what is the average
bra size

IS it normal for people
to have anal sex

It a guy pops a boner
what does a girl do

Can a Condom
get stuck in the
vagina during sex?

Can a girl piss ouT
her baby when she
is pregnant

Do animals have Bones
or periods

If a girl ~~is~~ has implants
Can she breast feed? and
also how does a girl
have a boner

Do ~~graph~~ guys.
have anything like
a period

when you have a
baby like in the
toilet and the baby
hits the water
instantly after its
born does it die???

could a woman get pregnant from a penis entering the butt

Do girls go into heat like dogs

is doggy style the most pleserable for guys? can you have an orgasum in the but? + Whats your favorite Posiston minus 69

when someone says
your loose - what does
that mean?

Do chickens
have foreskin?

how come girls always
like to smoke after
having sex?

can you still have
hunger when you're pregnant?

why do guys get boners

why do people have Migetts?

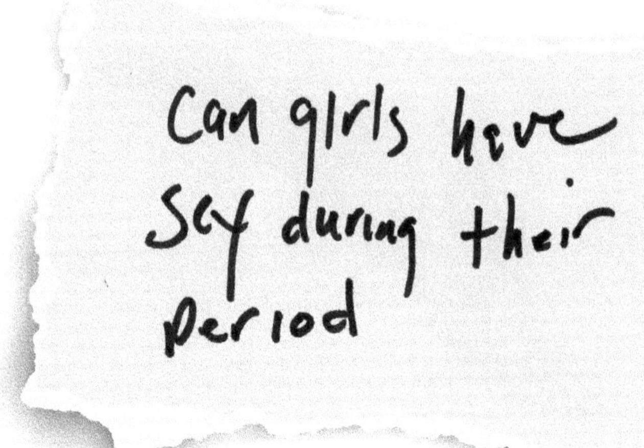
Can girls heve
sey during their
period

Is it possible to get
Aids/HIV through
grocery food that
is fresh

has anyone had chicken
pops twice?

how do lesbians have
~~stff~~ sexual intercourse

can static electricity
make your pubic hair
go up ↑ ↑ ↑ ↑

can semen get in through the ear?

What if you started making out with someone for a day and they had HIV/AIDS, would you get it

What happens to all of the millions of sperm thats floating around the Vagina

when a guy gets a
erection could they
stand on it

DO SPERM HAVE EYES
WHEN THEY SWIM to
THE EGGS ?

what if you
take viagra
on your penis

WHAT DoES a peNis
taste like for girls?

Please say my
name so people
Know whet I
think.   Doug

Does chocolate
make you
HORNY?

what happens
if you ~~cut~~ cut
your scrotum?
and can u
shave it?

What does penis
taste like Mrs. Tomlinson?

What would
happen if you
drink period
blood if you
thought it was
fruit punch?

How much semen do
guys usually ejaculate
each time

what will happen if you
Jack off to Much ! ! !

what does steriods
to your penis ?

why do people
masterbate?, Makes
no sense?

Will the penis get
cricket if you
masturbate to Much?

Do <u>you</u> recommend
Anal? and what is foreskin

can you pee
inside the vagina?

after girls give oral
sex do they get
penis breath?

are we going
to put condoms
on bananas

Does your pen,s
grow from
ejaculating
to much?

What is a quiet?

Is having an over
sized penis bad for
you?

If you take a
hole bottle of
viagra would
your penis burst

Is Male or female Masturbation better?

If you wear a
thong would it get
stuck in the vagina

what will happen if
a guy and a girl dog
or cat have sex — will
it get pregnant

Can a Penis have
a Penis wrinkle

I heard from someone you
can get pregnant
from eating a certain
Kind of FOOD

How many times do
you wipe your butt
after you go dookie?

IF two gay men
have sex cant the
one thats taking it
get pregnant

what happens if a dog haves
sex with a female or male
would the baby be deformed

can a girl get
horny from a
tampon?

What did the
pinus say to
the condom.

cover me i'm
going in

if I lite
My puebes on
fire will they
grow back

What is a love Nub?

*CAN the
condom GoME
in fruity
flavors*
(trix are for
Kids)

What would happen
If you pee in the womens
vagina while having sex?

if you have an outy
is it bad?

what would happen
if you use a
flashlight as a
sex tool

How can you tell when a
girl is horny or gets
a boner

do girls mastrubate
with dildos

q could you hide
things in a vagina

Do girls nipples
get hard when
they are horny?

how come
guys say
"give me head"

Can u get a boner while having sex?

Can Masturbation Affect your Mentality?

what do you call a lesbian dinosaur?

if you get nuttered
can doctors attach
the tubes back
together

what I learned is women
are like magic, they
make soft things hard and
get wet without water +
bleed without injury

What do you call
a mans jewels?
Testicks?

Whats the size of
a ~~the~~ normal vigina

What is the real name
for a boner and why
do they call it that

Why do you say girls
are supposed to be
developing breasts?
Some girls are flat

Do dogs get
"fixed" the same
as humans?

can you pop a
testicle?

Is the girls milk like
cow milk

Why do pinus stand?

THE END